A Hole in the Bottom of the Sea

Adapted by Jessica Law

Illustrated by Jill McDonald

Sung by The Flannery Brothers

Barefoot Books
step inside a story

There's a hole in the bottom of the sea.
There's a hole in the bottom of the sea.

There's a hole, there's a hole,
There's a hole in the bottom of the sea!

There's a **shark** in the hole in the bottom of the sea.

In the dark in the hole in the bottom of the sea.

There's a hole, there's a hole,
There's a hole in the bottom of the sea!

There's an eel
and a **shark** in the hole in the bottom of the sea.

He's **concealed**
from the **shark** in the hole in the bottom of the sea.

There's a hole, there's a hole,
There's a hole in the bottom of the sea!

There's a squid
and an **eel** and a **shark**
in the hole in the bottom of the sea.

Who hid
from the **eel** and the **shark** in the hole in the bottom of the sea

There's a hole, there's a hole,
There's a hole in the bottom of the sea!

There's a crab
and a **squid** and an **eel** and a **shark**
in the hole in the bottom of the sea.

Claws that grab
at the **squid** and the **eel** and the **shark**
in the hole in the bottom of the sea.

There's a hole, there's a hole,
There's a hole in the bottom of the sea!

There's a snail
and a **crab** and a **squid** and an **eel** and a **shark**
in the hole in the bottom of the sea.

Leaves a trail
past the **crab** and the **squid** and the **eel** and the **shark**
in the hole in the bottom of the sea.

There's a hole, there's a hole,
There's a hole in the bottom of the sea!

There's a weed
and a snail and a **crab** and a **squid** and an **eel** and a **shark**
in the hole in the bottom of the sea.

Grows at speed
past the **snail** and the **crab** and the **squid** and the **eel** and the **shark**
in the hole in the bottom of the sea.

There's a hole, there's a hole,
There's a hole in the bottom of the sea!

The sun feeds the weed feeds the **snail** feeds the **crab** feeds the **squid** feeds the **eel** feeds the **shark** in the hole in the bottom of the sea. (repeat)

There's a hole, there's a hole, There's a hole in the bottom of the sea!

So LOOK OUT if you go

to the hole in the bottom of the sea!

Blue Holes

There really are holes in the bottom of the sea! Blue holes are made when chemicals in the water dissolve the seafloor. The Great Blue Hole off the coast of Belize, in Central America, is the largest blue hole in the world. It is two hundred times deeper than an Olympic swimming pool!

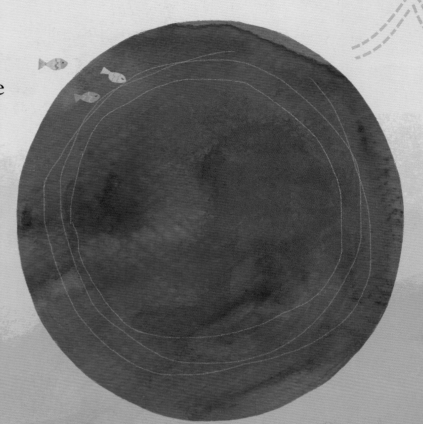

food chain

Who Eats Whom?

This picture shows how the food chain under the sea works. At the top of the chain are large meat eaters, or carnivores. These animals are predators; the smaller creatures they eat are their prey. Smaller carnivores eat herbivores, or plant eaters.

Herbivores eat the plants at the bottom of the food chain. Plants make their energy from sunlight.

The Ocean

The ocean becomes colder and darker the deeper you descend, as less and less sunlight can get through.

Sharks are fearsome predators. Most sharks have several rows of teeth; when the front row wears out, the row behind replaces it, so sharks' teeth are always razor sharp.

Eels hide in cracks on the sea floor, waiting to pounce on unsuspecting prey. There are many different kinds of eels. Moray eels are the biggest. They can grow to be longer than a small car!

Squids have beaks like a parrot! If they are chased, squids squirt black ink behind them from a special ink sac and escape while they are hidden by the inky water.

Crabs love to eat snails. Fiddler crabs have one giant claw for crushing the shells, and one tiny, sharp claw for cutting the food into small pieces — a bit like a Swiss Army knife!

Snails leave a trail of slimy mucus behind them to guide them home at the end of the day. Unlike snails who live on land, sea snails have eyes on their heads, not at the top of stalks.

Seaweed makes its own food from sunlight. Bladder wrack is a kind of seaweed that has pockets of air (like balloons). These pockets help it to float upright so that it can absorb as much light as possible.

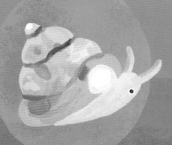

A Hole in the Bottom of the Sea

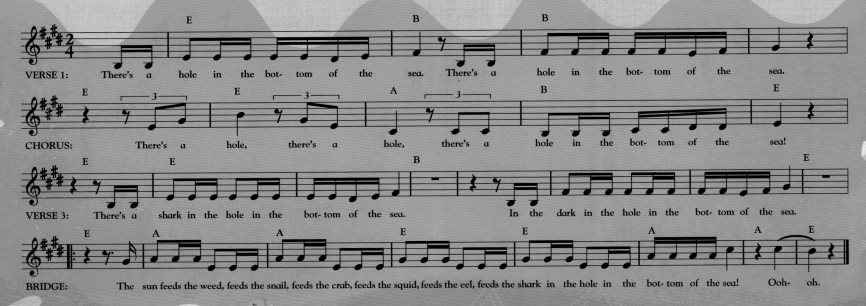

VERSE 1: There's a hole in the bot-tom of the sea. There's a hole in the bot-tom of the sea.

CHORUS: There's a hole, there's a hole, there's a hole in the bot-tom of the sea!

VERSE 3: There's a shark in the hole in the bot-tom of the sea. In the dark in the hole in the bot-tom of the sea.

BRIDGE: The sun feeds the weed, feeds the snail, feeds the crab, feeds the squid, feeds the eel, feeds the shark in the hole in the bot-tom of the sea! Ooh- oh.

Barefoot Books, 294 Banbury Road, Oxford, OX2 7ED
Barefoot Books, 2067 Massachusetts Ave, Cambridge, MA 02140

Text adaptation copyright © 2013 by Jessica Law. Illustrations copyright © 2013 by Jill McDonald
The moral rights of Jessica Law and Jill McDonald have been asserted
Music performed by Dan and Mike Flannery. Music arrangements copyright © The Flannery Brothers
Backing vocals by Clara Lofaro; trumpet by Jackie Coleman; saxophone by Mike Buckley;
trombone by Ric Becker; drums by Andrew Clifford
Recorded, mixed and mastered by Mike Flannery, New York City. Score transcribed by Jacob Lawson
Animation by Karrot Animation, London

First published in Great Britain by Barefoot Books, Ltd and in the United States of America by Barefoot Books, Inc in 2013
The hardback edition with enhanced CD first published in 2013. The paperback edition with enhanced CD first published in 2013
The paperback edition first published in 2013
All rights reserved

Graphic design by Penny Lamprell, Lymington, UK
Reproduction by B&P International, Hong Kong. Printed in China on 100% acid-free paper
This book was typeset in Carrotflower, Take Out the Garbage and Goudy Children
The illustrations were prepared in gouche and collage and assembled digitally in Photoshop and Painter

Hardback with CD ISBN 978-1-84686-861-0
Paperback with CD ISBN 978-1-84686-862-7
Paperback ISBN 978-1-84686-948-8

British Cataloguing-in-Publication Data: a catalogue record for this book is available from the British Library
Library of Congress Cataloging-in-Publication Data is available under LCCN 2012013763

7986